A LITTLE JAMIE BOOK

What It's Like to Be...

AMÉRICA FERRERA

Qué se siente al ser...
América Ferrera

BY/POR TAMMY GAGNE

TRANSLATED BY/
TRADUCIDO POR
EIDA DE LA VEGA

Mitchell Lane
PUBLISHERS

P.O. Box 196
Hockessin, Delaware 19707
Visit us on the web: www.mitchelllane.com
Comments? email us:
mitchelllane@mitchelllane.com

Mitchell Lane

PUBLISHERS

Printing   1   2   3   4   5   6   7   8   9

A LITTLE JAMIE BOOK

What It's Like to Be . . .	Qué se siente al ser . . .
America Ferrera	América Ferrera
The Jonas Brothers	Los Hermanos Jonas
Marta Vieira	Marta Vieira
Miley Cyrus	Miley Cyrus
President Barack Obama	El presidente Barack Obama
Ryan Howard	Ryan Howard
Shakira	Shakira
Sonia Sotomayor	Sonia Sotomayor

Library of Congress Cataloging-in-Publication Data
Gagne, Tammy.
  What it's like to be America Ferrera = ¿Qué se siente al ser America Ferrera? / by Tammy Gagne; translated by Eida de la Vega = por Tammy Gagne; traducido por Eida de la Vega.
    p. cm. — (A little Jamie book = un libro "little Jamie")
  English and Spanish.
  Includes bibliographical references and index.
  ISBN 978-1-58415-854-7 (library bound)
  1. Ferrera, America, 1984– —Juvenile literature. 2. Actors—United States—Biography—Juvenile literature. I. Vega, Eida de la. II. Title. III. Title: ¿Qué se siente al ser America Ferrera?
  PN2287.F423G34 2010
  791.4302'8092 — dc22
  [B]
                                                              2010006531

ABOUT THE AUTHOR: Tammy Gagne is the author of numerous books for both adults and children, including *What It's Like to Be Sonia Sotomayor* for Mitchell Lane Publishers. One of her favorite pastimes is visiting schools to speak to kids about the writing process. She lives in New England with her husband, son, dogs, and parrots.
ACERCA DE LA AUTORA: Tammy Gagne es autora de numerosos libros para niños y adultos, como *Qué se siente al ser Sonia Sotomayor* de Mitchell Lane Publishers. Uno de sus pasatiempos preferidos es visitar escuelas para hablarles a los niños acerca del proceso de la escritura. Vive en el norte de Nueva Inglaterra con su esposo, su hijo y algunos perros y cotorras.
ABOUT THE TRANSLATOR: Eida de la Vega was born in Havana, Cuba, and now lives in New Jersey with her mother, husband, and two children. Eida has worked at Lectorum/Scholastic, and as editor of the magazine *Selecciones del Reader's Digest*.
ACERCA DE LA TRADUCTORA: Eida de la Vega nació en La Habana, Cuba, y ahora vive en Nueva Jersey con su madre, su esposo y sus dos hijos. Ha trabajado en Lectorum/Scholastic y, como editora, en la revista *Selecciones del Reader's Digest*.
PUBLISHER'S NOTE: The following story has been thoroughly researched, and to the best of our knowledge represents a true story. While every possible effort has been made to ensure accuracy, the publisher will not assume liability for damages caused by inaccuracies in the data and makes no warranty on the accuracy of the information contained herein. This story has not been authorized or endorsed by America Ferrera.

PLB

What It's Like to Be...

AMERICA FERRERA

Qué se siente al ser...
América Ferrera

America Ferrera was born in Los Angeles, California, in 1984. Hers is now a household name, but for many years this talented actress went by her middle name, Georgina. It wasn't until she began acting that America started using her unusual first name.

América Ferrera nació en Los Ángeles, California, en 1984. América es ahora un nombre muy reconocible, pero durante muchos años, esta talentosa actriz era conocida por su segundo nombre: Georgina. Sólo empezó a usar su primer nombre cuando comenzó a actuar.

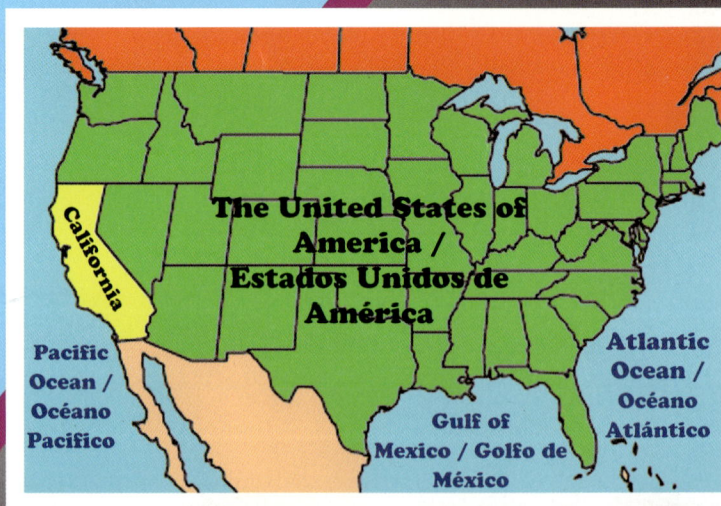

California

The United States of America / Estados Unidos de América

Pacific Ocean / Océano Pacífico

Gulf of Mexico / Golfo de México

Atlantic Ocean / Océano Atlántico

You may also know America by another name: Ugly Betty, the character she played on television. Every week millions of viewers tuned in to watch *Ugly Betty*, a show about a young journalist who works for a trendy fashion magazine. Transforming America into Betty Suarez wasn't easy. It took makeup artists and hairdressers several hours to complete the process.

Puede que también la conozcas por otro nombre: Ugly Betty (Betty, la fea), el personaje que interpretó en televisión. Semana tras semana, millones de televidentes sintonizaban Ugly Betty, una serie sobre una joven periodista que trabaja en una revista de modas. No era fácil transformar a América en Betty Suárez. Los maquillistas y peluqueros se pasaban varias horas en el proceso.

UGLY BETTY

ERIC

America has worked with some well-known actors in her short career. Besides *Ugly Betty* costar Eric Mabius (shown here), she has also worked with George Lopez, Wilmer Valderrama, and Forest Whitaker.

En su corta carrera, América ha trabajado con algunos actores muy conocidos. Además de Eric Mabius, con el que actúa en la serie (en la foto), también ha trabajado con George López, Wilmer Valderrama y Forest Whitaker.

America became very close with her *Ugly Betty* cast members. Although Becki Newton played Betty's rival on the show, in real life the two actresses are anything but enemies. Becki has said they often had a hard time keeping a straight face when their characters had to yell at each other on screen.

América está muy encariñada con los demás actores de Ugly Betty. Aunque Becki Newton era la rival de Betty en la serie, nada más lejos de lo que ocurre en la vida real. Becki ha dicho con frecuencia que le costaba mantenerse seria cuando ella y Betty tenían que gritarse en escena.

You may also know America from her role as Carmen in the wildly popular *The Sisterhood of the Traveling Pants* movies. Based on the books by Ann Brashares, the movies also star Alexis Bledel (next to America), Amber Tamblyn, and Blake Lively.

También puede que conozcas a América por su papel de Carmen en las popularísimas películas The Sisterhood of the Traveling Pants ("Verano en vaqueros"). En las películas, basadas en los libros de Ann Brashares, también actúan Alexis Bledel (junto a América), Amber Tamblyn y Blake Lively.

As a famous actress, América is often greeted by loads of adoring fans. They line up to get her autograph before she appears on shows, such as *The Late Show with David Letterman*.

Como es una actriz famosa, a América la saludan con frecuencia montones de admiradores. Hacen fila para obtener su autógrafo, cuando ella espera para presentarse en programas como The Late Show with David Letterman.

America and Amber Tamblyn listen as former first daughter Chelsea Clinton speaks about her mother's 2008 run for the presidency. America believes it is very important that young people vote. She has said, "We are the change we want to see in the world, but nothing will change unless we register and we vote."

América y Amber Tamblyn escuchan a la ex primera hija, Chelsea Clinton, mientras habla de la candidatura de su madre a la presidencia en el 2008. América cree que es importante que los jóvenes voten. Ha dicho: "Somos el cambio que queremos ver en el mundo, pero nada va a cambiar si no nos registramos y votamos".

AMERICA & HILLARY CLINTON

In 2007, the Writers Guild of America went on strike when the movie and television studios would not raise their pay. America and her *Ugly Betty* costars supported the writers' cause. Actors may get all the glory, but without writers, there would be no television shows like *Ugly Betty*.

En el año 2007, el Gremio de Escritores de Cine y Televisión de Estados Unidos se fue a la huelga porque los estudios de cine y televisión no querían aumentarles el salario. América y sus compañeros de reparto apoyaron la causa de los escritores. Los actores se llevan toda la gloria, pero sin los escritores, no habría series de televisión como Ugly Betty.

America adores her many young fans. They like posing for photos with her.

América adora a sus muchos admiradores. A ellos les gusta hacerse fotos con ella.

Part of America's job includes dressing up to attend fun celebrations—like the 22nd Annual Kids' Choice Awards. She and Chris Pine were presenters at the event.

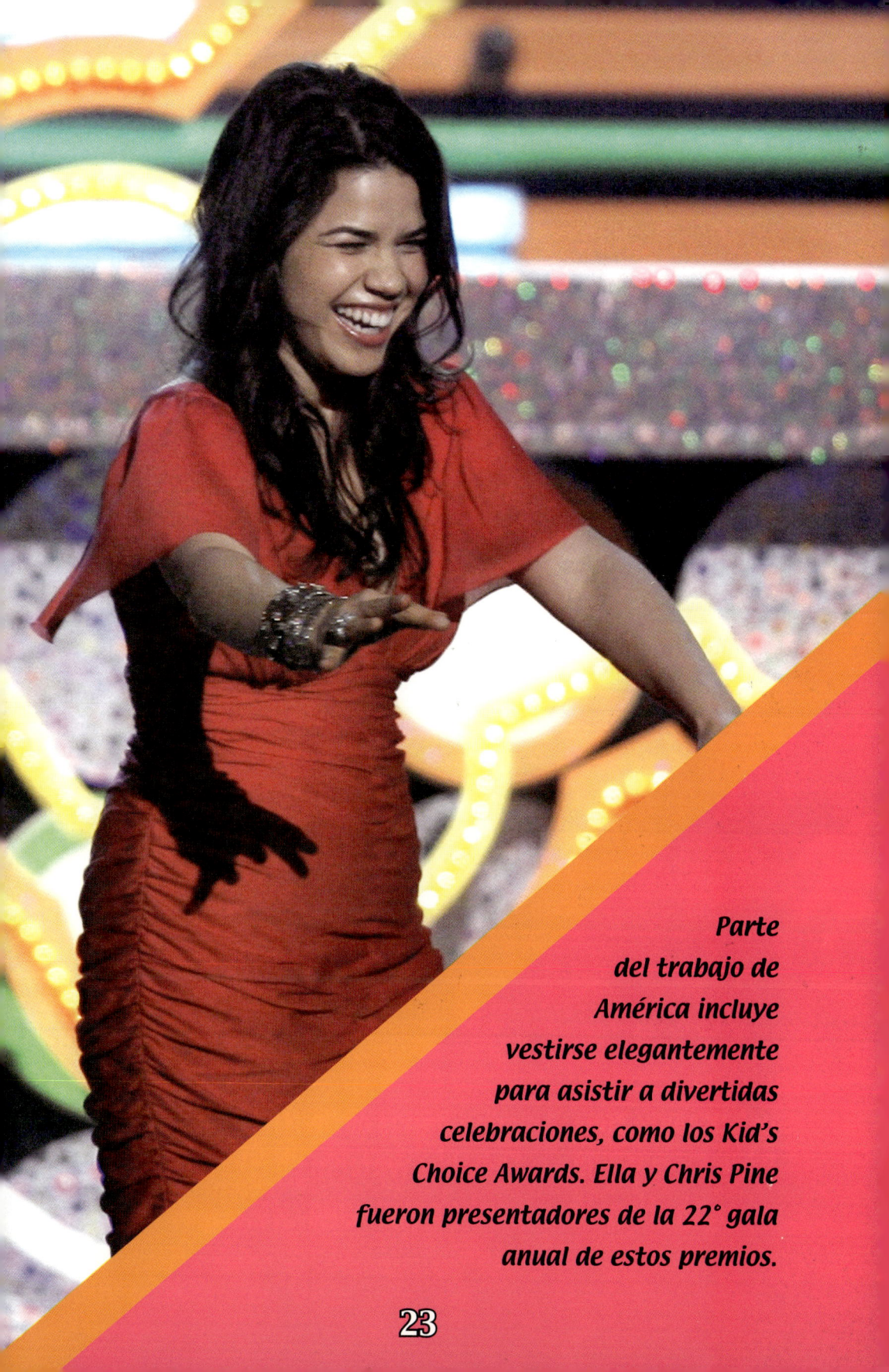

Parte del trabajo de América incluye vestirse elegantemente para asistir a divertidas celebraciones, como los Kid's Choice Awards. Ella y Chris Pine fueron presentadores de la 22° gala anual de estos premios.

In her spare time, America hangs out with her boyfriend, Ryan Piers Williams. They like watching basketball games when the New York Knicks are playing.

En su tiempo libre, América pasea con su novio, Ryan Piers Williams. Les gusta ver juegos de basquetbol cuando juegan los Knicks de Nueva York.

Sometimes America performs for charity events. In 2008, she hosted and sang at the 3rd Annual Hot in Hollywood benefit to help raise money for the AIDS Healthcare Foundation in Los Angeles. The event raised nearly half a million dollars.

En ocasiones, América actúa en eventos para recaudar fondos a favor de organizaciones de beneficencia. En el 2008, fue la presentadora y cantó en la tercera gala Annual Hot en Hollywood que ayuda a recaudar fondos para la AIDS Healthcare Foundation, una organización de Los Ángeles que ayuda a las personas con SIDA.

America's mother, who is also named America, moved to the United States from Honduras in the 1970s. She raised America and her five siblings all by herself. Now adults, each one has gone to college.

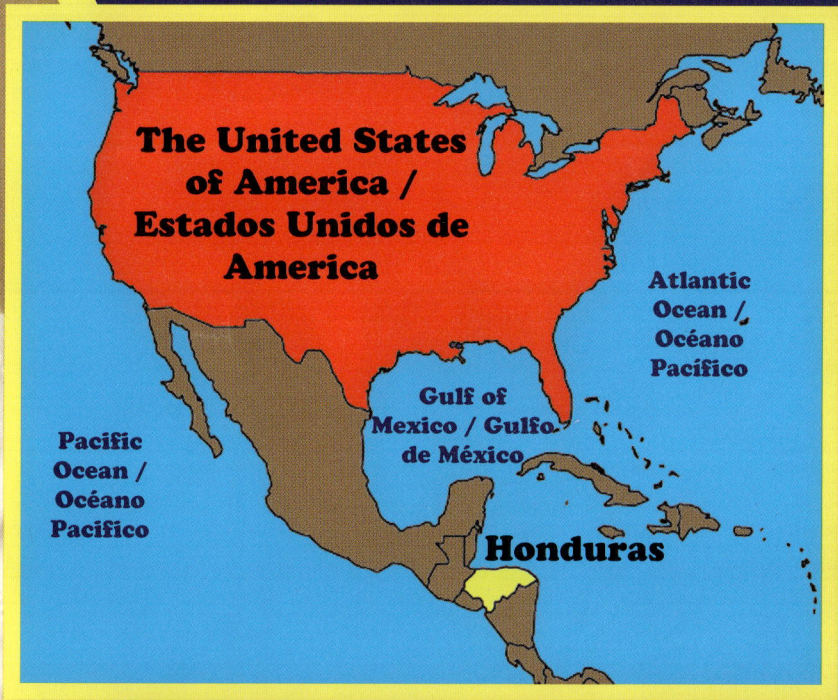

The United States of America / Estados Unidos de America

Atlantic Ocean / Océano Pacífico

Gulf of Mexico / Gulfo de México

Pacific Ocean / Océano Pacifico

Honduras

La madre de América, que también se llama así, es hondureña y vino a los Estados Unidos en la década de 1970. Ella sola educó a América y a sus cinco hermanos. Todos son ya adultos y todos han estudiado en la universidad.

Anything but ugly, America is a beautiful young woman with a lot of heart and talent. In addition to acting, she is also a producer and director. She has said that she loves being part of the creative process. Her exciting life leads many people to wonder—

"What's it like to be America Ferrera?"

América no es nada fea. Es una joven bonita con mucho talento y un gran corazón. Además de actuar, también es productora y directora. Ha dicho que le encanta ser parte del proceso creativo. Su vida llena de emociones hace que mucha gente se pregunte:

"¿Qué se siente al ser América Ferrera?".

FURTHER READING/LECTURAS RECOMENDADAS

Books/Libres

Anderson, Sheila. *America Ferrera: Latina Superstar*, Enslow Publishers: Berkeley Heights, New Jersey, 2009.

Works Consulted/Obras consultadas

Declare Yourself – http://www.declareyourself.com

Rodriguez, Marissa. "Wondrous Woman," *Hispanic*; October 2008, Volume 21, Issue 10, pp. 46–52.

"We The People," *Scholastic Scope*; September 15, 2008, Volume 57, Issue 2, pp. 14–16.

On the Internet

America Ferrera
http://www.americaferrera.org/

The Sisterhood of the Traveling Pants
http://sisterhoodofthetraveling pants.warnerbros.com/

Ugly Betty
http://abc.go.com/shows/ugly-betty

En Internet

América Ferrera
http://www.celestrellas.com/fotos/america-ferrera

INDEX/ÍNDICE